For the students I taught and experienced
stories with in Seoul, Kankakee, Oswego,
and Oak Brook. —JS

For Ms. Lynnie and Small World Early Learning.
And for Mrs. Simmers and Beechwood
Elementary. Thank you for creating communities
where children can explore and thrive! —VMJ

Text copyright © 2022 by John Schu. Illustrations copyright © 2022 by Veronica Miller Jamison. All rights reserved. No part of this book may be reproduced, transmitted, or stored in an information retrieval system in any form or by any means, graphic, electronic, or mechanical, including photocopying, taping, and recording, without prior written permission from the publisher. First edition 2022. Library of Congress Catalog Card Number 2021946699. ISBN 978-1-5362-0458-2. This book was typeset in Bembo Educational. The illustrations were done in watercolor, acrylic paint, and digital collage. Candlewick Press, 99 Dover Street, Somerville, Massachusetts 02144. www.candlewick.com
Printed in Humen, Dongguan, China. 22 23 24 25 26 APS 10 9 8 7 6 5 4 3 2

THIS IS A SCHOOL

words by
John Schu

illustrated by
Veronica Miller Jamison

CANDLEWICK PRESS

This is a kid.

This is a kid in a class. This is a class in a hall.

This is a hall in a school–

WELCOME!

Look.

Listen.

This is a place for discovery and
a time for asking questions:
big and small, silly and scary,
loud and quiet.

Sometimes we don't
have the answers.
Other days we just
feel stuck.

We ask.

We learn.

6 + 3 = 9

We share.

We help.

This is a community, growing.

Some days we get so excited and we can't wait to try something new.

We create.

We cheer.
We play.

We learn.

This is a community, celebrating.

Sometimes something happens,
and we can't all be together.

We learn.

We care.

We hope.

We heal.

This is a community, transforming.

Some people see what we're good at,
and that helps us to know it, too.

We speak.
We learn.

We grow.
We change.

This is a community, at work.

Some days we do the right thing . . .
and some days we definitely don't.

We fail.

We try.

We learn.

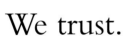

We trust.

This is a community, together.

Look.
Listen.

This is our class. This is our school:
librarians and coaches, helpers and staff,
principals and teachers, kids and friends.

And we are all important.